Anonymous

Report and Proceedings of Committee on Banking and Currency

Anatiposi

Anonymous

Report and Proceedings of Committee on Banking and Currency

Reprint of the original.

1st Edition 2023 | ISBN: 978-3-38230-844-5

Anatiposi Verlag is an imprint of Outlook Verlagsgesellschaft mbH.

Verlag (Publisher): Outlook Verlag GmbH, Zeilweg 44, 60439 Frankfurt, Deutschland
Vertretungsberechtigt (Authorized to represent): E. Roepke, Zeilweg 44, 60439 Frankfurt, Deutschland
Druck (Print): Books on Demand GmbH, In de Tarpen 42, 22848 Norderstedt, Deutschland

REPORT

AND

PROCEEDINGS OF COMMITTEE

ON

BANKING AND CURRENCY.

Printed by order of the Legislative Assembly.

TORONTO:

JOHN LOVELL, PRINTER, CORNER OF YONGE AND MELINDA STREETS.

1859.

LEGISLATIVE ASSEMBLY,

FRIDAY, 4*th March*, 1859.

Resolved, That a Special Committee be appointed to consider the subject of the Banking and Currency of the Province, to report from time to time; with power to send for persons, papers, and records.

Ordered, That the

HON. MR. GALT,
MR. SIMARD,
HON. MR. CAYLEY,
MR. BUCHANAN,
HON. MR. TERRILL,
HON. MR. BROWN,
HON. MR. DORION, AND
MR. HOWLAND,

Do compose the said Committee.

Attest,   W. B. LINDSAY,

Clerk Assembly.

———

ORDER OF REFERENCE.

THURSDAY, 17*th March*, 1859.

Ordered, That the subject of the state of trade and commercial depression be referred to the said Committee.

WEDNESDAY, 30*th March*, 1859.

Ordered, That the Bill (No. 131) to incorporate the Mechanic's Savings Bank of Toronto, (as amended by the Private Bill Committee) be referred to the said Committee.

REPORT.

COMMITTEE ROOM,
Wednesday, 27th April, 1859.

The Special Committee appointed to enquire into the working of the Banking and Currency system of this Province, and to whom was referred the enquiry into the causes of the late commercial depression, have agreed to the following, as their SECOND REPORT:

Your Committee, as a preliminary step to inviting the attendance of gentlemen practically acquainted with the subject referred, commenced their investigation by a series of questions submitted to the several Banks of the Province, and addressed circulars to numerous parties engaged in the commerce of the country. From the latter but few returns have as yet been received. The Banks, with one or two unimportant exceptions, have sent in replies more or less in detail.

The approaching close of the Session will necessarily interrupt the proceedings of your Committee, but they are so strongly impressed with the importance of the subjects referred, that they beg leave to recommend that a Committee be appointed to resume the enquiry in the ensuing Session of Parliament. It would also, in the opinion of your Committee, be productive of much advantage if the Government should see fit to appoint an unpaid commission to collect information from sources within the Province and elsewhere, during the recess.

Your Honorable House will not fail to observe that there is a strong concurrence of opinion amongst the Managers of these Institutions, that the Charters generally are defective in the safeguards attempted to be thrown around the paper circulation of the Province. This is a point of such vital importance, affecting the basis of the whole credit system, that it will doubtless engage the early attention of the Legislature.

The Circular addressed to the Banks, and the answers thereto, are submitted herewith, including the proceedings of the Committee.

The whole nevertheless humbly submitted.

WM. CAYLEY,
Chairman.

PROCEEDINGS OF COMMITTEE

ON

BANKING AND CURRENCY.

COMMITTEE ROOM,
FRIDAY, 11*th March*, 1859.

Committee met for organization.

PRESENT:

THE HON. MR. GALT,
" MR. CAYLEY,
" MR. TERRILL,
" MR. DORION,
" MR. BROWN, and
MR. BUCHANAN.

The Hon. Mr. *Brown* moved that the Hon. Mr. *Galt* do take the Chair.

Mr. *Galt* stated that his time being so fully occupied, he would beg leave to move in amendment, That the Hon. Mr. *Cayley* do take the Chair.— Which was carried.

The Chairman submitted a series of Questions which were read and agreed to, as follows:

Ques. 1.—Do the Bank Charters of the Province generally, by the privileges they confer and the limitations and conditions they impose, appear to you to provide for the several objects which it is presumed every Legislature has in view in sanctioning the establishment of such Institutions?

Ques. 2.—Do the Charters appear too restrictive or too unguarded, in any particulars?

Ques. 3.—What, in your opinion, is the *minimum* of Capital on which a Bank should be chartered?

Ques. 4.—Should there be a *maximum* limit?

Ques. 5.—Should the present restrictions, in regard to the nature of the securities upon which Banks are authorized to grant discounts, be retained or qualified?

Ques. 6.—What, practically, has been the effect of the late increased rate of interest which Banks are permitted to charge?

Ques. 7.—Would the interests of commerce, and the public advantage generally, be promoted by the removal of all restrictions as regards rates of interest?

Ques. 8.—What should be the *maximum* which a Bank should be allowed to issue of its own paper, with reference to its own capital?

Ques. 9.—What proportion should the specie and bullion in vault, bear to the paper circulation of a Bank?

Ques. 10.—In what year did the Bank with which you are connected commence operations, and with what capital?

Ques. 11.—What augmentation of capital, if any, has taken place since, and at what dates?

Ques. 12.—What dividends and bonuses has your Bank paid since its establishment?

Ques. 13.—State the amount of the Bank rest, in each year.

Ques. 14.—Has the Bank at any time suspended specie payments, and for what period?

Ques. 15.—What was the extent of the liabilities of the Bank at the time of suspension, the amount of specie in vault, and of discounted paper?

Ques. 16.—What was the state of the discount sheet, and the amount of Bank paper in circulation, at the resumption of specie payments?

Ques. 17.—What effect on the business transactions of the country was produced by the suspension and resumption of specie payments?

Ques. 18.—Have you any suggestions to offer with reference to the denominations of notes which now form the circulation; or with reference to the weekly settlement of balances between Banks?

Ques. 19.—Would it be desirable, in your opinion, to make silver a legal tender to a larger amount than it is at present, and to what extent?

Ques. 20.—Would a Provincial gold coinage be of advantage, and of what denominations?

Ques. 21.—Is any alteration desirable in the present mode of either receiving or paying out gold by tale or weight?

Ques. 22.—Referring to the commercial history of Europe and the United States, what do you find to have been the principal causes of commercial panics and depression?

Ques. 23.—Do you consider the same to have existed or to exist in Canada?

Ques. 24.—In your opinion. can commercial depression be alleviated, or overtrading checked, by Legislative action?

Ordered, That the said Questions be printed for the use of the Committee.

Adjourned to the call of the Chair.

Tuesday, 15th March, 1859.

The Committee met.

PRESENT:

THE HON. MR. CAYLEY, Chairman:
HON. MR. TERRILL, and
MR. HOWLAND.

The printed lists of questions were laid before the Committee.

The Chairman directed the Clerk to enclose two copies of the same to each of the several Banks in the Province.

Also, that 500 copies of the said list, with an additional heading, be printed and circulated, inviting information and opinions from the mercantile community and others, conversant with monetary transactions.

Adjourned to the call of the chair.

———

Monday, 4th April, 1859.

The Committee met.

PRESENT:

THE HON. MR. CAYLEY, Chairman;
HON. MR. GALT,
HON. MR. TERRILL, and
MR. SIMARD.

The Committee proceeded to consider Bill (No. 131) to incorporate the Mechanics' Savings Bank of Toronto referred to them, but from the absence of Mr. Howland, (a member of the Committee,) its consideration was postponed.

The Chairman laid before the Committee the replies received from several of the Banks.

Ordered, That the same be printed for the use of the Committee.

Adjourned until Wednesday at half-past ten o'clock, A.M.

———

Wednesday, 6th April, 1859.

The Committee met.

PRESENT:

THE HON. MR. CAYLEY. Chairman;
HON. MR. GALT,
HON. MR. DORION,
MR. HOWLAND, and
MR. SIMARD.

The Committee deliberated on Bill (No. 131,) to incorporate the Mechanics' Savings Bank of Toronto.

The Committee also deliberated on the Question of the Silver Currency in the Province.

Ordered, That the Clerk do lay before the Committee the Acts of Parliament on the Currency, and the Proclamation connected therewith, at its next meeting.

Adjourned to call of the Chair.

Saturday, 9th April, 1859.

The Committee met.

PRESENT :

THE HON. MR. CAYLEY, Chairman ;
HON. MR. GALT,
MR. HOWLAND, and
MR. SIMARD.

The Committee deliberated on Bill (No. 131) to incorporate the Mechanics' Savings Bank of Toronto.

The Committee deliberated on the question of Banking and Currency.

The Clerk laid before the Committee, a sketch of the Currency Acts.

Resolved, That the Committee adjourn until Tuesday next, at half-past ten, and that the Committee be specially summoned to consider the Bill (No. 131) to incorporate the Mechanics' Savings Bank of Toronto.

Tuesday, 12th April, 1859.

The Committee met pursuant to adjournment.

PRESENT :

THE. HON. MR. CAYLEY, Chairman ;
HON. MR. GALT,
HON. MR. TERRILL,
MR. HOWLAND, and
MR. SIMARD.

The Chairman submitted the following Report on Bill (No. 131) to incorporate the Mechanics' Savings Bank, Toronto.

The Committee on Banking and Currency to whom was referred the Bill to incorporate the Mechanics' Savings Bank, Toronto, beg leave to report :

That they have carefully considered the clauses of the Bill and compared them with the provisions of the General Savings Bank Act. The object of the Bill appears to be to remove to a great extent the restrictions imposed by the general Act with reference to the character of the securities which the contemplated Bank shall be authorized to hold.

Under the general Act, the Savings Banks, now in operation, are brought to a close in 1862, or are required to adopt an uniform and more stringent system with regard to the taking of securities. No impediment exists should the petitioners desire to incorporate themselves in accordance with the provisions of that Act.

To pass the Bill as prepared by the petitioners, is virtually to repeal the most important clause of the general Act which its framers had in view for the protection of the depositors.

Under these circumstances the Committee in reporting the Bill beg respectfully to state that in their opinion the preamble is not found.

At the same time entertaining strongly the conviction drawn from the past history of Savings Banks, that every protection should be afforded which the Legislature and State can throw around the middle and humbler classes who form the bulk of the depositors, they respectfully suggest that a broad and comprehensive scheme on the Savings Bank principle might be matured against the period when the existing charters shall expire to encourage as widely as possible among the humbler classes the desire to store up their earnings by extending to their deposits the guarantee of the Province.

Which was adopted, and

Ordered, That the Chairman do report the said Bill accordingly.

On motion of the Hon. Mr. *Galt*, it was

Resolved, That the Chairman do prepare a short Report, submitting the evidence and opinions of the Banks to the House ; also to suggest, as the Session was evidently drawing to a close, and little opportunity would be afforded of obtaining further information, that a Committee should again be struck next Session to resume the enquiry, and that it would be advantageous if the Government appointed an unpaid Commission during the recess to take evidence and collect information.

Adjourned to call of the Chair.

Wednesday, 27th April, 1859.

The Committee met.

PRESENT :

THE HON. MR. CAYLEY,
HON. MR. GALT, and
MR. SIMARD.

The Clerk reported that replies had been received from all the Banks to whom circulars had been sent, with the exception of two, (which replies are appended to the Report.)

The Chairman placed before the Committee a Draft Report, in accordance with the Resolution of the 12th April instant.

Ordered, That the same be considered at the next meeting of the Committee.

Adjourned to call of the Chair.

Thursday, 28*th April,* 1859.

The Committee met.

PRESENT:

THE HON. MR. CAYLEY, Chairman;
HON. MR. GALT,
MR. SIMARD,
MR. HOWLAND, and
MR. BUCHANAN.

The Chairman read to the Committee a Draft of a Report prepared in accordance with their instruction, and is as follows:

The Committee appointed to enquire into the working of the Banking and Currency system of the Province, and to whom was referred the enquiry as to the causes of the late commercial depression, have agreed to the following report:

Your Committee, as a preliminary step to inviting the attendance of gentlemen practically acquainted with the subjects referred, commenced their investigations by a series of questions submitted to the several chartered banks of the Province, and addressed circulars to numerous parties engaged in the commerce of the country. From the latter but few returns have as yet been received. The banks, with one or two unimportant exceptions, have sent in replies more or less in detail.

The approaching close of the Session will necessarily interrupt the proceedings of the Committee, but they are so strongly impressed with the importance of the subjects referred that they beg leave to recommend that a Committee be appointed to resume the enquiry in the ensuing Session of Parliament. It would also, in the opinion of the Committee, be productive of much advantage if the Government should see fit to appoint an unpaid Commission to collect information during the recess.

Your honorable House will not fail to observe that there is a strong concurrence of opinion amongst the managers of these Institutions, that the charters generally are defective in the safeguards attempted to be thrown around the paper circulation of the Province. This is a point of such vital importance, affecting the basis of the whole credit system, that it will doubtless engage the early attention of the Legislature.

The circular addressed to the Banks, and the answers thereto, are submitted herewith.

Mr. *Buchanan* moved that the said Report be amended by inserting the words, " from sources within the Province and elsewhere," after the word " information " in the second paragraph, which was agreed to.

The Hon. Mr. *Galt* moved the adoption of the same as amended,

Which was carried *nem. con.*

The Committee then considered the subject of the silver coinage in use in the Province, and after some discussion the Inspector General was requested to obtain the opinion of the Crown Officers with reference to certain points in relation thereto.

Ordered, That the Chairman do submit the Report as adopted together with the proceedings of the Committee to the House this day.

Adjourned *sine die.*

REPLIES APPENDED TO REPORT.

(From the Cashier of the Bank of Montreal,) Montreal.

To Question 1.—I am of opinion that very considerable changes in the charters of the Banks are called for, in order to secure for the Province a system of Banking established upon sound principles.

I consider the existing charters defective,—First, Because they empower the creation of capital for Banking purposes far beyond the wants of the country, and at the same time confer the privilege of issuing notes for circulation unaccompanied by any of those safeguards which are necessary for the public interests.

2d. Because they permit Banks to commence business upon too small an amount of paid up capital, and have not made provision for the bona fide payment of even the small amount required to be paid up. Some charters now exist under which an investment of $10,000 in debentures (being 10 per cent. upon what may be only a nominally paid up capital of $100,000) is all that is necessary to enable the Banks referred to, to issue notes to the extent of $110,000.

3d. Because there is no obligation on the part of the Banks to hold specie as a reserve against their liabilities, consisting of circulation and deposits.

4th. Because the Banks are not required to publish periodically the names of their partners, an obligation of great importance both as regards unpaid stock and the double liability of the shareholders.

To Question 2.—The answer to this question is embodied in that given to No. 1.

To Question 3.—I am of opinion that in order to ensure a system of Banking which will be attended with advantage to the Province, it is of the first importance that the Banks should have a large paid up capital.

The most successful Banks, and those which have conferred the greatest benefits upon communities, have been possessed of a large amount of capital.

No countries have benefitted more from their Banking institutions than Scotland and Ireland. In the former there are at present only fourteen Banks, and in Ireland seven.

In neither country is there any National Bank with the privileges of the Bank of England, and in neither can any new Bank of Issue be established.

The circumstances of Scotland and Ireland at no very distant period, were not dissimilar to those which now exist in Canada, and Banks established and conducted upon equally sound principles with those which have governed the monied institutions of those countries could not fail to confer inestimable advantages upon the Province.

The larger Banks in Canada have extended their business over the country, having at present seventy-four branches and agencies. Wherever they have found a favorable opening, they have planted an agency, so that there is not a District of any importance which does not enjoy all the advantages which Banking can confer, and at the same time the smallest agency possesses all the power and security of a large monied institution.

The circulating medium of the Province consists almost exclusively of the notes of the Banks, and it is of the greatest importance to the public interests that these institutions should be established upon a firm basis, which can only be secured by a large paid up capital. Hitherto, the issues of the Canadian Banks have commanded the highest degree of confidence, both in Canada and in the United States; and during the panic of 1857, they were received in that country with as much readiness as specie in payment of the notes which the local Banks were called upon to redeem.

This confidence in the stability of the Canadian Banks, can only be attributed to their large Capital.

Should small Banks be permitted to rise in Canada, I am of opinion they will prove an injury to the country.

The security they afford to the public is insufficient, and they cannot be conducted upon sound principles, and at the same time profitably. It will almost invariably be found that small Banks find it necessary to extend their business beyond the limits which prudent banking assigns, in order to meet their expenses and make a Return to the Shareholders.

During periods of stringency and pressure, small Banks find it difficult to meet their liabilities, and are unable to afford the assistance required by their customers and the public. The failure of one Bank would endanger every other and might be productive of most serious consequences.

The issues of small Banks frequently become discredited and the consequence is that the country where they exist becomes flooded with depreciated and unbankable currency.

Small Banks are generally defective in their management, they are controlled by a few who absorb their means, and thus comparatively little benefit is derived from such institutions by the communities in which they exist.

I am of opinion that the minimum capital should be one million of dollars. and that no Bank should be permitted to commence business with a smaller amount paid up than one third of its capital, and that it should be obligatory to pay up the whole within three years. Should the capital be larger than the minimum stated a proportionably longer time might be given for its payment.

To Question 4—As already stated I consider it of great importance, that the capital of the Bank should be large, and I believe that there is no reason to apprehend the establishment of Banks with too large an amount of capital.

To Question 5.—I am of opinion that the present restrictions should be retained, with this exception, that the Banks should be permitted to receive and hold Bills of Lading and Railroad Receipts representing property *in transitu*, as collateral security for Bills of Exchange or other obligations received in the ordinary course of business.

To Question 6.—No marked effect has been produced by the permission to charge the additional rate of one per cent. discount. The customers of the Banks, whose accounts are valuable, have not, I believe, been charged more than formerly, and the extension of the legal rate to 7 per cent, has scarcely afforded any inducement to grant accommodation unaccompanied by some collateral advantages.

To Question 7.—Decidedly so The limitation in the rate of discount chargeable by the Banks compels them to confine their advances to parties whose business affords some collateral advantages. The existing law is therefore inoperative as a means of really fixing and regulating the value of the money advanced by the Banks. Many classes who cannot offer the inducements alluded to are excluded from participating in banking facilities, and the direct benefits which should be open to all from the Banking Institutions of the country are confined to comparatively few. During periods of stringency and commercial difficulty, the effect of the Usury Laws is to render it necessary for the banking institutions to resort to expedients which are inconvenient to their customers. in order to keep their demands within proper bounds, such as peremptorily curtailing their accommodation, shortening the currency of bills, and charging high rates for exchange. Under such circumstances *inferior* customers have discounts refused altogether, while a *superior* class are only restricted in the facilities afforded them.

Parties keeping accounts valuable on other grounds, have in times of pressure a proportion of funds advanced to them in accordance with the Banker's estimate of the value of their accounts, while the applications of those, whose accommodation yields only the legal rate of interest are entirely rejected, and during the recent commercial crisis, when some restriction became necessary, had the Banks been permitted to charge a rate of discount in proportion to the actual value of money, many parties would have obtained facilities to whom they were denied.

The charge of a higher rate of discount would have had a decided tendency to reduce the amount of accommodation demanded by the more wealthy customers of the banks, and they would then have been enabled to spread their accomodation more generally; all classes of the commmunity would have received a more equal measure of support, and would have been better able to sustain the severe pressure, the greater benefit being experienced by the smaller than by the larger trader.

Experience has shown that the proper adjustment of the rate of interest is the true method of regulating the currency and credit of the country, and the community as well as the Banks suffered much during the late pressure in being compelled to keep the rate of discount at an unnaturally low level.

A moderate and temporary rise in the rate of discount can never inflict any real injury on trade, and would indeed be the means of saving parties from making great sacrifices in order to obtain the money they require. The power of demanding a higher rate of discount would be also beneficially used by the Banks, in checking speculation, and in giving warning of the approach of periods of difficulty, thus leading to a timely contraction of business, which would be attended with very important results.

This means of regulating the currency and credit of the country is especially necessary during a commercial crisis, and the necessity for keeping the rate of discount at an unnaturally low level has ever been found previous to a period of commercial difficulty, to produce a false security, causing engagements on credit to be maintained upon an undiminished scale, until the Banks for their own safety are obliged in the absence of any other check, to refuse accommodation, thereby inflicting serious injury upon trade.

The Banking institutions necessarily exert at all times a very important influence upon the general business of the country, and I believe that this can only be successfully done by a proper regulation of the rate of discount, both during periods of commercial prosperity and difficulty.

To Question 8.—I am of opinion that the issues of the Banks should not only be governed by the amount of paid up capital, but also by the reserve which they hold in specie.

I am of opinion that the privilege at present conferred upon the Banks of issuing paper for circulation is too extensive to be consistent with the safety of the monetary transactions of the country, while unaccompanied by those safeguards which experience has shown to be necessary.

The Banks furnish the circulating medium of the Province, and it is of the greatest importance that as much stability as possible should be given to their issues. No reserve of specie can insure the instant convertibility of all the notes of the Banks. The only security against an extraordinary demand, and for the notes of the Banks maintaining an equal value with gold, is the confidence of the public in the solvency of such institutions.

It is therefore of much importance that every reasonable precaution should be taken by the Legislature to secure that confidence. This, I believe, can be best accomplished by confining the privilege of issue to Banks having a considerable amount of paid up capital. But I am also of opinion that the Banks should be compelled to hold specie to the extent of not less than one fourth of their notes in circulation and one seventh of their deposits.

It will be the practice of every well managed Bank to keep not only a reserve in specie in proportion to its circulation and deposits, but also unemployed funds in the hands of its agents in London or New York. I am however of opinion that the Legislature in granting the valuable privilege of issue, should make it compulsory upon the Banks to hold a reserve in specie, and that the obligation should also extend to the liabilities of the Banks in the form of deposits.

The Banks are at present required to hold 10 per cent. of their paid up capital in Government Securities. This investment affords only a trifling security to the general creditors of the Banks, and is of no value as a reserve to meet any sudden demand or emergency, the securities not being at the disposal of the Banks, and if they were so, not readily convertible. Should the Banks be required to keep the reserve in specie, which has been mentioned, they might be relieved from the obligation to hold what is of so little practical value.

To Question 9.—The reply to this question has been given in the previous one.

To Question 10.—In 1817 with a capital of £250,000 of which £87,500 were paid in during the first year.

To Questions 11, 12 and 13.—The information is given in the annexed statement. (Page 9.)

To Question 14.—The Bank suspended specie payments upon the 18th May, 1837, and resumed upon the 23rd June, 1838. Again suspended in November, 1838, and resumed 1st June, 1839.

To Question 15.—At the first suspension the liabilities in circulation and deposits amounted to £388,000. The former amounted to £177,330. The Vault contained £56,457 in specie, and the amount under discount was £682,042.

At the second suspension the liabilities in circulation and deposits amounted to £386,652. The former amounted to £180,808. The Vault contained £117,623 in specie, and the amount under discount was £738,750.

To Question 16.—When the Bank resumed specie payments, in June, 1838, it had under discount £640,334 and the circulation was £209,353. On the second resumption it had under discount £653,833 and the circulation was £280,461.

To Question 17.—The suspension of specie payment was forced upon the Banks by the fears of the commercial community, their debtors, and had the immediate effect of depreciating the value of Bank Notes, then almost as now exclusively the circulating medium, and causing a rapid advance on the rate of sterling exchange, which reached a premium of 22 per cent, while to a considerable extent Banking facilities by a forced system of renewals, was confined to the class chiefly indebted to the Banks at the moment of suspension. The suspension had also the effect of raising the price of commodities in our own markets in proportion to the premium demanded for specie, all of which circumstances were no doubt injurious in their effects upon the commercial interest of the country, and would unquestionably have proved to a much wider extent disas trous, had it not been that simultaneously the enormous expenditure for military purposes, consequent upon the Rebellion, counteracted that result and rendered the resumption comparatively easy.

To Question 18.—I have no suggestions to make with reference to the denominations, of notes which now form the circulation. I consider them the most convenient for general use.

With regard to the settlement of balances between the Banks, I have to remark that the system organized among themselves has been found to work advantageously. It recognizes specie as the only proper basis upon which the balances can be adjusted, and it constitutes a valuable check upon imprudent Banking, and the over issue of notes.

The system, however, can only be maintained as a general Rule, while mutual confidence exists between the Banking Institutions. It has already met with interruption, in consequence of notes having been put in circulation, which the Banks have not felt it safe to receive. It is greatly to be regretted that un-bankable notes should begin to find a circulation in Canada.

To Question 19.—I am of opinion that no advantage would be gained by making silver coin a legal tender. The dollars and half-dollars of the United States, of certain weights and dates, are still a legal tender; but these coins have disappeared from circulation in consequence of their intrinsic value being relatively greater than that of the gold coins.

The British silver and Canadian coins in circulation are both depreciated in value, and to make either a legal tender would be in effect to alter the standard upon which the currency and all the monetary transactions of the country are based, and any measure having such an effect would be attended with injurious consequences.

To Question 20.—I am of opinion that it would be of no advantage what-ever. The Province can command at present an ample supply of gold upon the most favorable and economical terms; and any change in the present system would be detrimental to the public interests, as well as to those of the monied Institutions.

To Question 21.—I think not.

To Question 22.—Without entering into the history of the periods, referred to, it may be stated that the monetary crises which have occurred, have been chiefly produced by speculation and over-trading.

To Question 23.—To somewhat similar causes may be traced the depressed state of trade now existing in Canada. As will generally be found to to be the case, it was preceded by a period of unwonted expansion and apparent prosperity.

An outlay of millions of foreign capital in the course of a few years upon Public Works, together with high prices of bread-stuffs, had the effect of stimu-lating every branch of trade to an unprecedented degree.

The expenditure of all classes throughout a large section of the country was characterized by extravagance, and a spirit of speculation also pervaded the com-munity, which had the effect of diverting a large amount of capital from the legitimate purposes of trade and agriculture.

The expenditure upon Public Works was curtailed in 1857 and nearly ceased during 1858, and the country was thus deprived of valuable resources. The harvest in 1857 was deficient, and that of 1858 still more so. The actual loss from the failure of the crops during two successive years must be estimated at a very large sum.

To these circumstances, following upon a period of extraordinary activity in trade, during which large importations took place, must be attributed the commercial and agricultural distress under which the Province is now suffering.

To Question 24.—I am of opinion that no legislative action can alleviate the depression which now prevails, but I believe that much may be done to check future over-trading by the adoption of measures calculated to insure the solvency and prudent management of Banks of Issue. I am also of opinion that were the restrictions removed which the Usury Laws impose upon the Banks, these institutions would have it in their power to afford a large measure of support during monetary crises, and would, by a proper regulation of the rate of discount, exert a beneficial influence, in anticipation of such periods of commercial difficulty, by checking speculation and contracting the operations of trade.

(Signed,)   D. DAVIDSON,
Cashier Bank of Montreal.

Montreal, 28th March, 1859.

BANK OF MONTREAL.

Statement of Paid up Capital, Dividends and Contingent Fund, from 1817 to 1858.

	1817—18	1818—19	1819—20	1820—21	1821—22	1822—23	1823—24	1824—25	1825—26	1826—27	1827—28	1828—29	1829—30	1830—31
Paid up Capital	87,500	162,500	187,500	187,500	187,500	187,500	187,500	187,500	187,500	187,500	187,500	212,500	212,500	250,000
Dividends....Per cent.	3	8	6½	5	6	6	6	6	3	None.	None.	2½	6	6
Contingent Fund	None.	1,042	1,957	1,501	4,420	5,863	7,657	7,695	3,016	13,308	26,771	21,823	7,840	16,898

	1831—32	1832—33	1833—34	1834—35	1835—36	1836—37	1837—38	1838—39	1839—40	1840—41	1841—42	1842—43	1843—44	1844—45
Paid up Capital	250,000	250,000	250,000	250,000	250,000	250,000	391,372	422,262	433,869	500,000	500,000	617,062	669,417	750,000
Dividends....Per cent.	7-5 Bonus	8-6 Bonus	8-6 Bonus	8-6 Bonus	8-4 Bonus	8	6-16 bon. on old Stock.	7	6	6	7	7	6	7
Contingent Fund	18,530	21,913	21,827	90,165	27,250	49,457	11,499	20,717	22,370	38,654	50,000	45,000	53,700	70,976

	1845—46	1846—47	1847—48	1848—49	1849—50	1850—51	1851—52	1852—53	1853—54	1854—55	1855—56	1856—57	1857—58
Paid up Capital	750,000	750,000	750,000	750,000	750,000	750,000	750,000	885,990	992,670	1,000,000	1,257,625	1,377,430	1,439,845
Dividends....Per cent.	7½	7½	7	6	6	6	6½	7	7	7½	8	8	7
Contingent Fund	82,625	76,000	15,250	19,055	30,048	54,088	80,598	106,217	171,320	212,500	175,000	185,000	185,000

The following answers received—

(From the Cashier of the Bank of Upper Canada,) Toronto.

To Questions 1 and 2.—Many of the objects which the Legislature has had in view in granting charters to banking institutions have undoubtedly been attained, such as the supplying a circulating medium more convenient than specie, facilitating the daily transactions of the community, and economizing the use of money by means of bankers' drafts, and book credits. Some of the precautionary clauses, however, and especially in the more recent charters might in my opinion be improved.

The minimum of paid up capital might be raised, and the regulations affecting the issue of paper money made more stringent without inconvenience to, and more thoroughly securing the public.

Too great care cannot be taken to insure the integrity of the money basis on which our paper circulation and the credit system of the country rest.

To Question 3.—Between $800,000 and $1,000,000 is little enough for a minimum limit.

To Question 4.—From five to seven millions is an ample capital for the present state of the community.

To Question 5.—Banks should be authorised to take bills of lading and railroad and warehouse receipts.

To Question 6.—The period during which the law has been in force is too short to afford a practical test, but I apprehend that the imposition of any limit on the procurement of money must defeat the objects for which the law was framed, that of checking over speculation and affording relief to the trading community in periods of commercial difficulty.

To Question 7.—All restrictions should in my opinion be removed; when money is abundant the limit of seven per cent. will scarcely ever be reached, except in cases where the transactions are to be extended over a lengthened period, which cannot strictly be classed under the head of banking operations. When money is tight the limit operates as an entire exclusion of a certain class of customers. Fluctuations in the rates of discounts are evidences of changes in the supply of the money market. When left free, a steady rise will give a reliable indication of coming stringent times. The imposition of a limit leaves the public without warning, until the banks taking alarm, withhold or greatly curtail their discounts, when in too many cases the refusal to discount is attributed to any but the right cause.

The complaint is frequently made that Banks give a preference to wealthy and independent customers. The limit naturally produces such a result. In England when Bankers find themselves called upon to curtail their discounts, the object is carried into effect by raising the rate, and thus by checking speculation reduce the number of customers, leaving those only as applicants whose necessities compel them to give the higher rate. But if instead of this mode of curtailing discounts, bankers are left to select which of their customers they will supply, they will naturally prefer those, whose punctuality is the most assured, whose need probably is the least, or cases from which by drawing exchange or otherwise they may expect to derive some incidental advantage, while it is evident that speculation will not be restrained so long as there is a class of customers who can enjoy the advantage of obtaining money from the bank at six or seven per cent at a time when its value in the market is ranging possibly from nine to twelve. It is unnecessary for me to remark that many parties who have thus been excluded from Bank accommodation by the operation of the limit, have been driven to pay from one to two per cent. per month for temporary loans in other quarters.

To Question 8.—The present restrictions afford scope enough, perhaps too great, in the absence of any regulations with regard to the proportion of specie to be kept by the Bank.

To Question 9.—This will in some measure depend upon the amount of funds held in London or in the United States on which the Bank can draw. One-fifth might be considered a safe limit. The amount of deposits should also be kept in view. Paper money has no intrinsic value, its credit and value are derived from the confidence the public possesses that it is convertible into specie on demand. It is not necessary that the whole of the circulation should be represented by specie to ensure this, but enough should be kept in reserve together with the power of drawing exchange to guard against exhaustion. It may be taken for granted that under no circumstances can the entire paper circulation of a country be forced back upon the Banks. But should the public become apprehensive of the stability of any particular Bank of issue, the paper of that Bank will be forced in, and its place supplied by the others.

To Question 10.—In 1822 the charter was obtained authorizing a capital of £200,000 the amount paid up was £10,341.

To Questions 11, 12, 13.—Will be found in the annexed statement (page 13.)

To Question 14.—The Bank suspended specie payments on the 5th March, 1838, and resumed them on the 1st November 1839.

To Question 15.—Circulation £117,005
Deposits 34,595
Specie in vault 63,013
Discounted paper 212,864

To Question 16.—Discounted paper £304,068
Specie in Vault 82,782
Circulation........................... 186,382

To Question 17.—The suspension of specie payments produced a great rise in prices, and in the value of exchange.

To Question 18.—The denominations in use appear to be adapted to the purposes of the community. In London the balances are settled daily at the clearing house and after setting off the various drafts and orders for transfer held by the banks, one against the other, the ultimate differences are settled by drafts on the Bank of England, where all the bankers kept account and where a special account is opened for the business of the clearing house; exchequer bills have also been used in settling balances. In this province, where we have neither exchequer bills nor a chief bank of issue, and where the amounts to be adjusted are held principally in the notes of the respective banks, the ultimate balances are generally settled in specie or its equivalent in exchange. Under these circumstances I am not prepared at present to suggest a change of system.

To Question 19.—Not to any considerable extent, and only in our own coin. At the present time Canada notes are more in demand in several of the neighbouring States of America than their own, and are used as a means of drawing exchange and gold from Canada. A moderate per centage, say five per cent., payable in specie would have the effect of equalizing the value of the paper circulation, and remove the inducement which now exists for picking up Canada notes.

To *Question* 20.—Yes, of equal fineness with American gold in four and two dollar pieces.

To *Question* 21.—Sovereigns of full weight should be received and paid out by tale. Light sovereigns should be treated as bullion.

To *Question* 22.—Excessive speculations, over-trading, and the abuse of credit.

To *Question* 23.—I have no doubt of it. The large expenditure upon our Railroads and public works, and the great influx of foreign capital between 1852 and 1856 induced extravagant speculations, and excessive prices to be given for wild lands; schemes for new villages and towns were set afloat in every direction; mercantile transactions were carried to an extent far beyond the wants of the country, and bank accommodation was pressed to its utmost limit. Then came a revulsion. The large expenditures on Railroads and the foreign supplies were cut off or greatly diminished. The land speculations had absorbed the means of many a farmer and diverted them from the proper cultivation of his farm. Then followed two years of bad crops, and on the back of all, the commercial crisis in the United States which extended to Europe, and seriously aggravated the general depression under which the province was labouring.

To *Question* 24.—In so far only as a sound banking system, and a well regulated currency may operate as a check to rash speculations and the abuse of credit.

(Signed,)   THOS. G. RIDOUT,
Cashier.

Bank of Upper Canada,
   Toronto, 26th March, 1859.

ANSWER TO QUESTIONS Nos. 11, 12 AND 13.

STATEMENT shewing the yearly amounts of the paid up capital; also, the dividends, bonuses and rests from the commencement of this institution—in July, 1822—to the 1st of January, 1859.

Yearly Periods	Capital Stock Paid Up	Dividends		Bonuses		Bank Rests	Remarks
		Rate	Amount	Rate	Amount		
1823, June 30	£10,640	5	£523			£161	
1823, Dec.31	13,415	8	493			148	
1824, do	28,181	8	1,624			431	
1825, do	37,030	8	2,333			316	
1826, do	54,037	8	3,863			1,928	
1827, do	63,250	8	4,813	6	£3,793	2,609	
1828, do	72,410	8	5,790			5,082	
1829, do	76,903	8	6,036	6	6,000	8,187	
1830, do	100,000	8	7,574			5,253	
1831, do	100,000	8	8,000	12 & 6–18	18,000	9,810	
1832, do	100,000	8	8,000			256	
1833, do	183,241	8	12,264			6,992	
1834, do	200,000	8	15,695	4	8,000	8,469	
1835, do	200,000	8	16,000			5,959	
1836, do	200,000	8	16,000			12,555	
1837, do	200,000	8	16,000			15,512	
1838, do	200,000	8	16,000			17,551	
1839, do	200,000	8	16,000			13,227	
1840, do	200,000	8	16,000			24,163	
1841, do	200,000	8	16,000			27,463	
1842, do	200,000	8	16,000	10	20,000	26,605	
1843, do	223,270	6½	12,617			4,918	
1844, do	244,951	7	15,171			9,094	
1845, do	270,660	7	18,041			12,006	
1846, do	307,338	7	20,154			12,964	
1847, do	375,303	4	23,851			11,028	
1848, do	380,761	4½	15,159			5,660	
1849, do	380,810	5½	17,135			9,583	
1850, do	380,922	6	20,949			10,514	
1851, do	381,236	6	22,570			18,466	
1852, do	420,128	7	24,041			30,051	
1853, do	497,393	7	31,346			68,414	
1854, do	409,163	8	34,921	11¼	62,500	55,348	
1855, do	607,612	8	47,688			76,438	
1856, do	721,870	7	54,146			70,000	
1857, do	777,017	8	53,634			80,000	
1858, do	780,170	8	62,302			70,843	
			£679,913		£118,293		

BANK OF UPPER CANADA,
Toronto, March 26, 1859.

(Signed,) THOS. G. RIDOUT, Cashier.

The following answers received—

(From the Cashier of the Commercial Bank of Canada,) Kingston.

To Question 1. — This query involves the whole question of banking in Canada, but I may briefly state, that I consider the restrictions and conditions imposed upon the chartered Banks (except the smaller institutions lately chartered) provide fully for the safety of the public. As regards the privileges conferred upon the chartered Banks, their usefulness to facilitate trade is materially affected by the tax on circulation, and the limitation of rate of interest they are allowed to charge, and the risk of loss arising from transactions during the periodical crises of trade, counterbalance the privileges of the Banks to an extent not generally understood.

To Question 2.—I am of opinion, as stated above, that the Bank charters are sufficiently guarded, and that in respect of tax on circulation, rate of interest to be charged, the nature of securities which may be taken, and obligation to hold a large sum of Provincial Debentures, they are unnecessarily restrictive.

To Question 3.—In my opinion, no Bank should be chartered with a smaller capital than one million dollars, nor allowed to go in its operation until at least one half the capital has been subscribed, and one fourth paid up.

To Question 4. - I regard four million of dollars as sufficient capital for a Bank in Canada, at present, reference being had to the Banks now in existence, and to other reasons. I think no Bank should be chartered with a larger capital than six million of dollars.

To Question 5.—I am of opinion that Banks should be authorised by law to take any kind of securities as collateral for debts or advances.

Were the present restrictions removed it would be well to have a legal form for taking securities other than personal, containing power of sale on due notice and other necessary provisions.

To Question 6.—Sufficient time has not elapsed since the late increase in rate of interest allowed on Bank transactions, to judge correctly of its effects. The low rates of interest which have ruled in Great Britain and the United States, together with the comparatively reduced business of Canada generally have rendered the period exceptional so to speak.

But so far as my own observation has extended, the increased rate of interest has enabled parties to get loans, which otherwise would not have been given. All mercantile people are, however, satisfied that the increase was too small to give effectual relief, and as a necessary consequence, no material reduction in the high rates paid by borrowers to private lenders has been effected.

To Question 7.—An experience of upwards of twenty years has satisfied me that the interests of commerce and of the public would be promoted by the removal of all restrictions on rates of interest: The course of the money market in London during the crisis of 1857 sufficiently proved this beyond all question: and the restrictions in force in Canada greatly aggravated the effects of that crisis in this country.

To Question 8. — In my opinion no Bank should be allowed to issue its notes beyond the amount of its paid up capital. Any excess should be only when based upon specie in vault to a corresponding amount—dollar for dollar— in addition to ordinary reserves of gold, as stated below.

To Question 9.— The specie in vault should never be less than one fifth of the notes in circulation, and generally I should say one-fourth was the better rule.

To Question 10.—The Commercial Bank of Canada commenced business in 1832, with a capital of £100,000.

To Question 11.— The capital was increased to £200,000 in 1836, to £500,000 during the years 1844 to 1853, inclusive, and to £1,000,000 in the years 1855 to 1858, inclusive. The capital is now all paid up.

To Question 12.—The dividends have been as follows:

1833	December,	4 p. ct.	1842	July,	4 p. ct.	1851	January,	3 p. ct.
1834	June,	4 "	1843	January,	4 "	"	July,	3 "
"	December,	4 "	"	July,	4 "	1852	January,	3 "
1835	June,	4 "	1844	January,	3 "	"	July,	3 "
"	December,	4 "	"	July,	3 "	1853	January,	3½ "
1836	June,	4 "	1845	January,	3 "	"	July,	3½ "
"	December,	4 "	"	July,	3½ "	1854	January,	3½ "
1837	June,	4 "	1846	January,	3½ "	"	July,	3½ "
"	December,	3 "	"	July,	3½ "	1855	January,	3½ "
1838	June,	3 "	1847	January,	3½ "	"	July,	4 "
"	December,	4 "	"	July.	3½ "	1856	January,	4 "
1839	November	4 "	1848	January,	3½ "	"	July,	4 "
1840	January,	4 "	"	July,	3½ "	1857	January,	4 "
"	June,	4 "	1849	January,	3 "	"	July,	4 "
1841	January,	4 "	"	July,	3 "	1858	January,	4 "
"	July,	4 "	1850	January,	3 "	"	July,	4 "
1842	January,	4 "	"	July,	3 "	1859	January,	4 "

The bonuses have been, 6 per cent. in 1838; 10 per cent. in 1843.

There was also a stock bonus of one share of stock at par for each three shares held, or a money bonus of 8 per cent. in lieu of such one new share at par. The shareholders generally took shares and not money.

To Question 13.—The reserve fund in each year has been as under:

	£	s.	d.	
In 1834	3,158	9	4	
1835	4,098	15	8	
1836	174	15	6	Bonus £6000 paid.
1837	2,240	16	5	
1838	7,407	17	7	
1839	11,754	1	9	
1840	20,194	17	9	
1841	25,280	14	5	
1842	29,452	6	5	
1843	31,291	5	11	
1844	7,992	18	1	Bonus £20,000 paid,
1845	14,818	7	10	[1843.
1846	18,436	17	4	
1847	19,010	0	11	
1848	22,427	7	3	

1849	22,427	7	3
1850	24,000	0	0
1851	28,000	0	0
1852	30,000	0	0
1853	41,620	7	4
1854	64,457	9	10
1855	78,508	1	5
1856	101,116	17	7
1857	120,263	2	6
1858	150,000	0	0
1859	150,000	0	0

To Question 14.—The Bank, in common with all the Banks in Canada and the United States, suspended specie payment in 1837.

To Question 15.—The liabilities of the Bank at the time of suspension amounted to £155,544 0 10 currency. The specie in vault was £17,327 6 1, and the amount of discounts was £283,976 1 8.

To Question 16. — On resumption of specie payments, the amount of the discounts was £398,691 18 11 and the amount of Bank notes in circulation £236,686 10 0.

To Question 17.—The suspension of specie payments in Canada, rendered necessary by concurrent suspension in the United States and by the rebellion, enabled this Bank, with others in Canada to afford the requisite facilities to its customers and to the public, which, had specie payments been compulsory, could not have been done, and the trade of the country must have been reduced practically to barter. So soon as the state of the country admitted it, specie payment was resumed and then no practical injury or check to trade resulted from resumption. A temporary rise in sterling exchange was the only inconvenience of importance to individuals, arising from suspension.

To Question 18.—The denominations of Bank notes now forming the circulation of the Banks in Canada are just what the business of the country requires. Different localities and kinds of business require notes of different value, and no new regulation of a legislative nature should be made on this subject. The Banks will furnish just such notes as are best suited to the wants of the community.

As regards settlement of weekly Bank balances it can generally be made without having recourse to specie, but in order that every Bank may hold proper reserves and keep its business in a sound state and within limits proportioned to its capital, it is indispensably necessary that final settlements between Banks, (such as now prevail at Montreal where nearly all settlements terminate) should be made on the basis of specie and nothing else. The system of settlement in use in Montreal has been attended with the best results. In Scotland reserves are held in part, and settlements made by Government Exchequer bills, but obviously such securities could not be introduced into settlements of Canada because they could not be converted into gold when necessary, without loss, either in Canada or New York. There are numerous objections also to any fixed regulations for settlement of balance by Exchange on London or on New York.

To Question 19.—I am of opinion that it would not be desirable to make silver a legal tender to an amount exceeding ten dollars.

To Question 20.—I consider the general interests of the province and of the Banks do not require a provincial gold coinage. The Banks could not hold reserves in such coin. Reserves must be in coins of the United States or Sovereigns, so the surplus fund may be sent to New York without loss, or if a supply is needed it may be got from thence at all times.

To Question 21.—I consider no alteration in the existing regulations for receiving and paying gold is required.

To Question 22.—Over-trading, or in other words, too extended credit, has been the principal cause. Short crops always materially aggravate panics and depression in trade.

To Question 23.—Over-trading, and particularly speculation in unproductive real estate, existed in Canada to a great extent during the years 1854, 1855, 1856 and 1857. Subsequently the effects have been severely felt. At present, from the causes named, and deficiency of last harvest, business generally has been much reduced.

To Question 24.—I am of opinion that generally, no legislative action can wholly check over-trading, or materially alleviate commercial depression ; but a good bankrupt law would act as a check on excessive speculation, and be an important protection to trade ; such have been the effects of the bankrupt law in Great Britain.

> I have the honor to be,
> Sir,
> Your most obedient servant,
>
> (Signed,)   C. S. ROSS.

Kingston, 21st March, 1858.

———

The following answers received—

(*From the Manager of the Bank of British North America*), *Kingston.*

To Question 1. Assuming that the several objects which every Legislature has in view in sanctioning the establishment of Banks are at all times of a safe and legitimate character, I consider that the present Bank Charters do in the main provide for those objects, though I do not doubt that some improvements might be introduced.

To Question 2. Too restrictive in some respects, and too unguarded in others.

To Question 3. In my opinion no Bank should be entitled to go into operation unless it have a paid up capital of at least One Million of dollars.

To Question 4. I think there should be.

To Question 5. They should be retained.

To Question 6. On the part of some at least of the Banks, there has been a disposition, in regulating their charge for interest, to consider the nature of each transaction and the position of the money market. On the part of the public, I have not noticed any expression of dissatisfaction when the increased rate has been adopted. This Bank has not yet found it necessary to charge more than six per cent. for advances made in the ordinary way of business for respectable and punctual customers.

To Question 7. They would in my judgment be best promoted by the adoption of a maximum rate (say 10 per cent.,) sufficiently high to attract capital to the Province in the worst times, but not so high as to be a means of extortion under any circumstances. Whatever rate might be fixed upon, no individual nor Corporate body should be privileged to charge more than another.

To Question 8. This question cannot be properly answered unless there be also taken into account the amount of deposits held by the Bank and the extent to which both branches of liability (I mean circulation and deposits) are used by the Bank as capital for loaning purposes. I see no reason for putting a limit on either the issues or the deposits of a Bank. The danger lies in the extent to which the floating capital arising from these sources might be employed in making advances to the community. It therefore appears to me that instead of limiting the issues it would be more effectual to put some restriction on the power of making loans, confining the amount to a sum proportioned to the paid up capital stock. If it be asked, what this proportion should be? I answer that in my judgment the amount under loan at any one time should never be more than double that of the paid up stock.

To Question 9. Here again the deposits should be considered in connection with the circulation, both equally requiring a specie reserve. I am of opinion that one-third of the united amount should be held in specie if we would avert undue pressure in troublous times.

To Questions 10 *to* 17 *inclusive.* Answers to these questions can be best obtained from the General Manager of this Bank.

To Question 18. I have no suggestions to offer regarding the denominations of notes. Settlements between Banks should be compulsory whenever demanded by the creditor, and should always be in specie if required.

To Question 19. I think it would not be desirable.

To Question 20. A Provincial gold coinage might be rather advantageous than otherwise, provided the intrinsic value of each coin were precisely that of coins current in the United States, and bearing the same denomination. If this principle were departed from, a Provincial coinage would only work confusion and would be better dispensed with. The denominations should be $2, $5, $10, $20. Coins like the quarter-eagle, containing a fractional part of a dollar, should be excluded. I am of opinion that the gold coinage of the United States should still be retained as a legal tender, even though a Provincial coinage were introduced.

To Question 21. I think not.

To Question 22. The extravagant and complicated system of credit which generally prevails, especially that credit which is based upon the deposits held and the notes issued by the various Banks.

To Question 23. I think the same causes have existed, and still exist in Canada, though not to so great an extent as in the United States.

To *Question* 24. In my opinion they might be by increasing the privileges but restraining the powers granted to Banking Corporations, allowing them to charge higher rates of interest when necessary, but restricting them to a more moderate use of their floating capital.

As my reasons were not asked for, I have confined myself as nearly as possible to what appeared to be the desire of the Committee—a simple expression of opinion on the points raised.

I am, Sir,
Your obedient servant,

(Signed)   S. TAYLOR,
Manager.

(From the General Manager of the Bank of British North America,) Montreal.

To *Question* 1.—They do not.

To *Question* 2.—The charters appear to be too unguarded in several important features.

To *Question* 3.—A bank ought not in my opinion to receive a charter unless one million dollars of capital be subscribed : Four hundred thousand dollars of this capital ought to be paid up before the bank is allowed to go into operation, and in order to be assured that the bank has this capital paid up, the whole amount ought to be deposited in the hands of the government to be returned to the Bank when it commences business. Unless some measure of this kind be adopted, the public can never have a guarantee that any portion of the capital of a Bank has been paid up, and it is almost certain that in the majority of instances in the case of small banks the notes of stockholders will be discounted and renewed for the purpose of giving the Bank a nominal capital. The whole capital of the Bank ought to be paid up within five years from the date when it commences business in equal annual instalments. A list of Stockholders with their addresses and amount of stock subscribed by each ought to be furnished to Government before the charter is granted and a yearly statement of the same nature sent. The Charter ought to be forfeited in the event of the whole of the stock not being paid up within the prescribed time. All the Directors ought to be British subjects. The number of Branches and Agencies ought to be limited by the amount of paid up capital—say a Branch or Agency for each two hundred thousand dollars paid up.

To *Question* 4.—I consider that six million dollars ought to be the maximum limit to the capital of a Bank in this country.

To *Question* 5.—The present restrictions with regard to the nature of securities upon which Banks are allowed to grant discounts or make advances may be safely qualified. In the Charters of most of the local Banks a clause has been introduced which renders it illegal for these institutions to make advances upon the security of any goods, wares or merchandize. This clause prevents Banks holding Bills of Lading or Warehouse Receipts as collateral security. The restriction is an inconvenient one and might be removed with advantage to the public and the Banks.

To Question 6.—The business of the Province has been so much depressed and the rate of interest in London and New York has been so unprecedentedly low since the Usury Laws were altered that the effect of the modification has not been properly tested. Several of the Banks in the Province have not availed themselves of the privilege of charging a higher rate of interest than six per cent, unless in very special cases.

The Bank capital now at disposal of the community is quite equal to all legitimate demands.

To Question 7.—Yes they would.

To Question 8.—A Bank ought not to be allowed to issue a larger amount of its paper than the paid up capital of the Bank amounts to.

To Question 9.—Every Bank should be required to retain a reserve of specie equal to one third of its circulation and one sixth of its deposit accounts and deposit receipts (or special deposits). It would not however be expedient to introduce any clause into the charter of a Bank which would involve its immediate forfeiture if the amount of its specie in vaults where reduced below the specified proportion. But as it is highly desirable and very important that the issue of paper money by the banking institutions shall have a sound specie basis it might be enacted that when a Bank allows its specie to fall under the required amount as compared with its liabilities, the amount of liabilities not protected by the requisite specie reserve shall be chargeable with interest at the rate of ten per cent. per annum with one per cent. additional for each month that the specie reserve is deficient.

This charge to be considered as a fine and to be paid to the Government. The charter of the Bank to be forfeited in the event of the specie reserve being deficient for the period of one year. A statement of the position of the Bank every fortnight ought to be sent to Government and published in the Gazette. It may not be out of place to extract here from the annual message of the President Buchanan to Congress, 7th December 1857, the following paragraphs :

" It is one of the highest and most responsible duties of government to in-
" sure the people a sound circulating medium, the amount of which ought to be
" adapted with the utmost possible wisdom and skill to the wants of internal
" trade and foreign exchanges. If this be either greatly above or greatly below
" the proper standard, the marketable value of every man's property is increased
" or diminished in the same proportion, and injustice to individuals as well as
" incalculable evils to the community are the consequence."

" Unfortunately, under the construction of the federal constitution, which
" has now prevailed too long to be changed, this important and delicate duty has
" been dissevered from the coining power, and virtually transferred to more
" than fourteen hundred State Banks acting independently of each other, and
" regulating their paper issues almost exclusively by a regard to the present in-
" terest of their stockholders. Exercising the sovereign power of providing a
" paper currency, instead of coin for the country ; the first duty which these Banks
" owe to the public is to keep in their vaults a sufficient amount of gold and
" silver to insure the convertibility of their notes into coin at all times and under
" all circumstances.

" *Banks Specie Basis.* No bank ought ever to be chartered without such
' restrictions on its business as to secure the result. All other restrictions are
" comparatively vain. This is the only true touchstone, the only efficient regu-
" lator of a paper currency,—the only one which can guard the public against
" over-issues and Bank suspensions."

" Each of our fourteen hundred banks has but a limited circumference for
" circulation, and in the course of a very few days the depositors and note hold-
" ers might demand from such a Bank a sufficient amount in specie to compel it
" to suspend even although it had coin in its vaults, equal to one third of its imme-
" diate liabilities."

" And yet I am not aware, with the exception of the Banks of Louisiana, that
" any State Bank throughout the Union has been required by its Charter to keep
" this or any other proportion of gold or silver, compared with the amount of its
" combined circulation and deposits. What has been the consequence? In a
" recent Report made by the Treasury Department on the conditions of the Banks
" throughout the different States, according to Returns dated nearest to January
" 1857, the aggregate amount of actual specie in their vaults is \$58,349,838,
" of their circulation \$214,778,822 and of their deposits \$230,351,352. Thus it
" appears that these Banks in the aggregate have considerably less than one
" dollar in seven of gold and silver compared with their circulation and deposits."

" It was palpable therefore that the very first pressure must drive them to
" suspension and deprive the people of a convertible currency with all its disas-
" trous consequences."

The State Bank of Missouri ought also to have been excepted. They as well
as the Banks of Louisiana are required to retain one-third of the amount of
their circulation in specie. It is worthy of note—that the Banks in these States
did not suspend during the crisis of 1857, and the people were spared many of
the evils caused by the mismanagement and imprudence of the Banks in the
other States of the Union.

To Question 10.—The Bank of British North America commenced operations in 1836 with a capital of one million pounds sterling, which is all paid up.

To Question 11.—None.

To Questions 12 *and* 13.—See separate statement, (page 24.)

To Question 14.—When the Banks suspended specie payment on the 18th
May, 1837, in consequence of the suspension of the Banks in the United States and the failure of the London agents of most of the Banks in this country,
the Bank of British North America had not issued any notes and had only about
£20,000 in deposits which it held at the disposal of the depositors, in specie. Until
the resumption of the other Banks on the 23rd June, 1838, this Bank received and
paid the notes of the other Banks, and therefore it did not suspend specie payments.
When the political disturbances in Canada were renewed in 1838, an order in
Council was passed authorising the suspension of all the Banks in Canada. The
Bank of British North America suspended specie payments on the 6th November,
1838, and resumed on the 1st June, 1839.

To Questions 15 and 16.—See separate statement, (page 25.)

To Question 17.—The crisis of 1837 in England and the United States
and the political disturbances which then broke out in Canada had a very depressing effect upon the commerce of this country, and would have caused much embarrassment had it not been for the large expenditure by the British Government
in Canada. I do not think that the suspension of the banks had a prejudicial
effect upon the business of the country. The banks conducted their affairs with
great caution and prudence and resumed without the least inconvenience either
to themselves or their customers. As the Government duties required to be

paid in specie, some inconvenience was at first experienced by the mercantile community in providing specie to pay customs duties; this, however, was soon overcome as specie became an article of merchandize bearing a premium of from two to eight or ten per cent.

To Question 18.—I have not. The present denomination of notes in circulation, are in my opinion convenient. The mode of settlement with banks in specie which we now have cannot be improved, and it is highly desirable that it should be continued.

To Question 19.—I believe there can be no objection whatever to allow silver to be a legal tender along with gold, provided if the former be not a depreciated coin as compared with the latter. For instance Spanish, Mexican, and American dollars are a legal tender at present for any amount, but as these coins bear a premium of from one to fifteen per cent, they are exported and sold. It would be highly objectionable and inexpedient to make any silver coins or tokens a legal tender, which by Legislative enactment are made to bear a higher than their intrinsic value. If such coins were made a tender for a much larger amount than ten dollars it would have the effect of depreciating the currency to an indefinite extent, the depreciation increasing as the coins or tokens became worn, and in proportion to the amount put into circulation.

If the Colonial silver coins which have been lately issued were made a legal tender for much more than ten dollars, and the amount issued were greater than what the community required as small change, the currency would become immediately depreciated as compared with that of the United States at least four per cent, and the rates of exchange in New York and Britain would rise in the same ratio.

To Question 20.—A provincial gold coinage would not, in my opinion be of the least advantage to the country, but the contrary. The gold coins of the United States are the most convenient for the Banks to retain as their reserves, and the supply of a gold coinage would only entail a needless expense upon the Government.

To Question 21.—No alteration is desirable.

To Question 22.—The question is of so comprehensive a character that I cannot at present answer it as fully as I would wish. When personally examined, I will give particulars in a more detailed manner than I now do.

The panics and commercial depressions in England have been brought about by several causes, but principally by bad crops, short supplies of cotton, mismanagement and failure of unsound Banks, and derangement of the monetary affairs of the United States. The last named was one of the chief causes of the commercial crisis of 1837–42, and was altogether the cause of the panic and monetary crisis of 1857, aggravated, no doubt, by the failure of the Western Borough and New Castle and Durham Banks.

The periodical panics to which the United States are subject must be attributed mainly to the unsoundness of its banking system, the inflation of the currency, and to the extravagance and speculative character of the people.

To Question 23.—Commercial crisis and depressions in trade in Canada have been chiefly caused by derangement in the monetary affairs in Britain and the United States, by bad crops, and by a falling off in the demand for the staple products of the country—timber, ships, ashes, grain, &c. The depression which now exists in this country has been caused by the bad crops of the past two years, and it has been aggravated by too extensive credit having been given and taken by all classes of the community. No doubt it has also been increased by the panic of 1857.

In Western Canada, where the depression has been most felt, credit has been extended too much. The farmers, receiving cash for nearly all they sold, ought not to have taken credit for nearly all they bought.

There can be but little doubt that notwithstanding the abundant crops of 1853, 1854, and 1855, and the high price obtained for agricultural produce, the farmers, as a class, are more deeply indebted in 1857 than they were in 1853. Any irregularity or embarrassment in the finances of the agricultural population of Canada, constituting as it does two-thirds of the whole population, must of course have a very depressing effect upon the trade of the country. Many of the farmers have very much improved their position by bringing under cultivation a greater breadth of land, and providing themselves with improved agricultural implements, &c., which of course adds to the productive power of the property, but as a class their expenditure has been too great, on dress, living, &c.

The cessation of the large expenditure upon Railroads and public works has been a great cause of disturbance in the monetary affairs of the province. While the expenditure lasted, prices were inflated, land attained to a fictitious value, speculations were entered into which became ruinous to those engaged in them, and excessive importations were stimulated.

The bad crops of the last two years, and the expenditure on public works having in a great measure ceased, will account for the depression which now exists in this country.

To Question 24.—Governments can do much by wise legislation and by encouraging a sound banking system to check over trading and alleviate commercial distress.

As bearing upon the subject, I beg to give an extract from the last annual report of the able Superintendent of the banking department of the State of New York.

" One of the causes which tended to produce the suspension of 1857, the " superintendent believes and so stated in his report of that year, was the multi- " plicity of banks of small capitals. Still he believes the bank capital of the " State smaller than is required by the usual business of our citizens. Their relief " cannot be looked for in the multiplication of small banks, but in raising the " capitals of these already in existence, when located in places where increasing " business warrants additional bank facilities. The superintendent looks upon the " direction taken by the increased bank capital of the State this year, as adding " more to the stability and prosperity of the business men and to the banks them- " selves, than when he was starting twenty-five or thirty new institutions a year " with two or three times the amount of additional capital."

The opinions of this gentleman are corroborated, I find, by most of the superintendents of the Banking Department of the United States, and by many reflecting and intelligent persons who have devoted their attention to this subject.

(Signed,)   J. M. PATON,
General Manager.

Bank of British North America,
Montreal, 31st March, 1859.

N.B.—There are sixteen Banks in Scotland, with a capital of £9,345,000 sterling paid up. There are eleven Banks in Canada with a capital of upwards of $20,000,000. The population of Scotland is about a third more than Canada, its trade, commerce and manufacturing interests, &c., immeasurably greater.

To Question 12.—Since its establishment in December, 1836, it has paid as follows, viz :

No. of Dividend.	Date when declared.	Per cent, half-yearly.
1	July, 1838,	3
2	January, 1839,	3
3	July "	3
4	January, 1840,	$2\frac{1}{2}$
5	July, "	$2\frac{1}{2}$
6	January, 1841,	$2\frac{1}{2}$
7	July, "	$2\frac{1}{2}$
8	January, 1842,	3
9	July, "	3
Additional Dividend paid in additional shares given to certain shareholders.	1843,	$2\frac{1}{2}$
10	March, 1843,	3
No Dividend.	July, "	
11	March, 1844,	2
12	September, "	2
13	March, 1845	2
14	September, "	$2\frac{1}{2}$
15	March, 1846,	$2\frac{1}{2}$
16	September, "	$2\frac{1}{2}$
17	March, 1847,	$2\frac{3}{4}$
18	September, "	3
19	March, 1848,	3
20	September, "	$2\frac{1}{2}$
21	January, 1849,	$2\frac{1}{2}$
22	July, "	$2\frac{1}{2}$
23	January, 1850,	$2\frac{1}{2}$
24	July, "	$2\frac{1}{2}$
25	January, 1851,	$2\frac{1}{2}$
26	July, "	$2\frac{1}{2}$
27	January, 1852,	$2\frac{1}{2}$
28	July, "	3
29	January, 1853,	3
30	July, "	3
31	January, 1854,	3
32	July, "	$5\frac{1}{2}$ Bonus of $2\frac{1}{2}$ p. ct. included.
33	January, 1855,	3
34	July, "	6 Bonus of 3 p. ct. included.
35	January, 1856,	3
36	July, "	6 Bonus of 3 p. ct. included.
37	January, 1857,	3
38	July, "	6 Bonus of 3 p. ct. included.
39	January, 1858,	3
40	July, "	3
41	January, 1859.	3

To Question 13.—   Sterling,   £   s.   d.
31st December 1837.. 20,334   6   8
                    1838................................. 19,642   3 10
                    1839................................. 22.362   6 11
                    1840................................. 29,458 15   4
                    1841................................. 31,441 10 10
                    1842................................. 18.909 15 10
                    1843................................. 20,529 11   5
                    1844................................. 30,439 14   1
                    1845................................. 36,733 10   1
                    1846................................. 61,457   8   6
                    1847................................. 55,502 11   6
                    1848................................. 57,302 18   7
                    1849................................. 58,359 10   9
                    1850................................. 59,542 10   3
                    1851................................. 75,221 13   6
                    1852................................. 84,698 12   2
                    1853..This includes bonus of £30,000
                            paid in 1854.............. 125,349 10   0
                    1854..   do   1855 140,041   7   2
                    1855..   do   1856 145,117   9 10
                    1856..   do   1857 146,061   8   4
                    1857..No bonus paid 120,768   6   1
                    1858..Not yet received.

To Question 15.—Statement of Assets and Liabilities at suspension on 6th November, 1838.

    Liabilities :
    Deposits bearing interest...................... $128708.00
    Deposits not bearing interest..................   186767.00
    Circulation....................................   116311.00

                                     $431786.00

    Assets :
    Local Bills discounted.................... ....$1240990.00
    Specie..   124276.00

                                       $1365266.00

To Question 16.—Statement of Assets and Liabilities at the resumption of specie payment on 1st June 1839.

    Liabilities :
    Deposits bearing interest...................... $211071.00
    Deposits not bearing interest..................   249233.00
    Circulation....................................   170817.00

                                       $631121.00

    Assets :
    Local Bills discounted.......................$1098333.00
    Specie..   144133.00

                                       $1242466.00

                              T. PATON,
Bank of British North America,   General Manager.
    Montreal, 6th April, 1859.

The following answers received :—

(*From the Manager of the Bank of British North America,*) *Toronto.*

To Questions 1 *and* 2.—I cannot answer these questions, not having copies of all the charters of the Banks of the Province.—It is generally understood that charters, too unguarded in many particulars, have been granted

To Question 3.—In my opinion, the minimum capital of a Bank not having Branches or Agencies should be £100,000—and of a Bank having Branches and Agencies £250,000. It is to be regretted that by the present law facilities are afforded for the establishment of small Banks. During commercial panics and depression, small Banks, instead of being a benefit to a country, increase the general ruin, either by failure, or by rendering it necessary for the large Banks, from prudential motives, to sustain them, thereby depriving themselves of the means of adequately assisting their own customers. All classes of society are deeply interested in maintaining the high character to which the chartered Banks of this country have attained, and care should be taken in granting charters, that the control of the currency, *to any extent*, should not be placed in the hands of irresponsible parties.

To Question 4.—It is not important that there should be.

To Question 5.—Not having copies of the several charters of the Banks, I cannot answer this question. But I think that all Banks should be put upon the same footing as to restrictions, if any, in regard to the nature of the securities upon which they grant discounts.

To Question 6.—It has, to some extent, enabled the Banks to grant accomodation to the mercantile and agricultural community which otherwise would not have been extended. (This Bank, Bank of British North America, since the passing of the Act, in August last, amending the laws of the Province regulating the rate of interest, has not, except in a few cases, charged the increased rate of interest.)

I may here remark that it is generally admitted that if the Act above referred to, removing restrictions as regards rates of interest, that may be exacted by individuals, and which induced parties to send capital for investment in this country, had not been passed, there would have been much greater depression and distress in Western Canada during the past winter.

To Question 7.—They undoubtedly would.

To Question 8.—An answer to this question would be merely an opinion and not founded upon any principle that I know of. It might be safe and prudent to allow Banks, the liability of whose shareholders is unlimited, to issue notes to the full amount of their paid up capital. Cases might arise, however, where it would be neither safe nor prudent to grant this privilege.

To Question 9.—Not less than one-fourth.

To Questions 11, 12, 13, 14, 15, 16 *and* 17.—These questions will be answered by the General Manager of this Bank. I was not in this country during the suspension of specie payments.

To Question 18.—No notes of a less value than $4 should be issued. All arrangements regarding the settlements of balances between Banks should be left to the Banks themselves to settle.

To Question 19.—In my opinion it would not.

To Question 20.—A Provincial Gold Coinage to take the place of the notes under $4 in value, withdrawn, would be of advantage.

To Question 21.—I am not aware of any alteration being desirable.

To Questions 22 *and* 23.—The causes of commercial panics are generally attributed to sudden checks given to an extensive trading upon credit. In Canada before the late panic occurred, from the effects of which the country has not yet recovered, trade received a stimulus from the large outlay in Railroads and other works, and also from the high prices of farm produce. The latter no doubt induced parties to purchase lands at ruinously high prices and led to speculative transactions which have brought ruin upon many. Canada must always suffer from commercial panics in other countries.

Her merchants, as a general rule, carry on business far beyond the power of their capital, and the country is at all times largely indebted to England, the United States and other countries, so that when a panic arises abroad, the effects are immediately felt in this country.

To Question 24.—In my opinion commercial depression cannot be alleviated by Legislative action. Over-trading, however, might be checked by that means, but the remedy would be fatal to the prosperity and progress of the country. The remedy to which I refer is the withdrawal of all paper money and the substitution of a metallic circulating medium. The effects of this would be to limit the commercial transactions of the country to little more than its actual capital.

W. G. CASSELS,
Manager.

Bank of British North America,
    Toronto.

——————

The following answers received—

(*From the Quebec Bank,*) *Quebec.*

To Question 1. They do.

To Question 2. Yes, too restrictive in compelling the Banks to invest in Government securities one-tenth of the capital subscribed and paid up previously to the passing of the Act.

To Question 3. Two hundred and fifty thousand pounds.

To Question 4. Of four million dollars.

To Question 5. Restrictions should be retained.

To Question 6. Beneficial.

To Question 7. Not as regards Banks.

To Question 8. Amount of paid up capital and specie on hand.

To Question 9. About one-eighth or one-tenth.

To Question 10. 1818.   Capital £75,000.

To Question 11. In 1841. Augmentation of £25,000.
In 1853. Further augmentation of £150,000.

To Question 12. Six to eight per cent. per annum including Bonuses.

To Question 13. The surplus fund or rest in

1822...	£786	19	10	1835...	£15937	16	7	1847...	£7234	11	9
1823...	569	15	0	1836...	1149	16	6	1848...	13746	19	7
1824...	1673	16	11	1837...	2974	2	7	1849...	7162	9	1
1825...	2188	9	9	1838...	832	15	10	1850...	6956	8	8
1826...	4586	17	3	1839...	4189	11	4	1851...	6056	1	7
1827...	220	9	0	1840...	6197	2	7	1852...	1502	5	1
1828...	714	13	3	1841...	2733	1	11	1853...	5634	1	9
1829...	1749	5	10	1842...	4621	11	2	1854...	15686	0	10
1830...	2193	7	10	1843...	2896	2	9	1855...	16839	7	11
1831...	5700	18	10	1844...	4221	12	1	1856...	29453	2	0
1832...	6242	14	2	1845...	3710	4	5	1857...	14032	11	4
1833...	6410	13	3	1846...	4517	5	10	1858...	23584	2	11
1834...	10844	11	10								

To Question 14. Yes, from 17th May, 1837, to 26th May, 1838.

To Question 15. Amount of liabilities................... £85,123 0 8
Do.   specie in vault......   1,900 9 6
Do.   discounted paper... 142,028 1 1

To Question 16. Discount sheet amounted to £122,680 1 4
Bank paper in circulation........... 64,010 10 0

To Question 17. Favorable.

To Question 18. None.

To Question 19. Yes, to the extent of forty dollars.

To Question 20. It would be, provided that the standard was made equal to the Sovereign or American.

To Question 21. None.

To Question 22. Over-trading.

To Question 23. It has existed, but not so at present time.

To Question 24. No.

C. GETHING,
Cashier, Quebec Bank.

The following answers received—

(From the Manager of the Quebec Bank,) Toronto.

To Question 1.—Yes, generally, with some exceptions.

To Question 2.—Too unguarded in some of the late charters.

To Question 3.—I think there should be a paid up capital of £100,000 before going into operation.

To Question 4.—I think not.

To Question 5.—It would be an accommodation to the public, as well as a safety to the Banks, if a greater latitude were allowed us in taking securities.

To Question 6.—It appears to have had the effect of reducing the rate of interest generally.

To Question 7.—I have no doubt of it.

To Question 8.—The present regulation, I think, is fair.

To Question 9.—About a fourth or fifth; or available funds in New York.

To Question 10.—In 1818. I am not aware with what capital.

To Question 11.—I must refer you to our Head Office for the dates. A Bill was pased last session to increase our capital to £750,000.

To Questions 12, 13, 14, 15, 16, 17, 18.—I must refer you to our Head Office.

To Question 19.—When gold is at a premium in the States, the money brokers there make a regular business of collecting our notes, bring them over here, and demand gold for them. This is done to a considerable extent, and drains the country of gold.
If silver was a legal tender to a larger amount, we could pay in that coin, which would soon put a stop to it.

To Question 22.—Over-trading and speculation, which was also the cause of our present depression.

To Question 24.—I fancy not.

W. H. RANSOM,
Manager Quebec Bank, Toronto.

The following answers received—

(From the President of the City Bank,) Montreal.

To Question 1.—In most particulars, they do. Charters should permit Banks, however, to increase or decrease their rates of discount according to the market value of money, as the Bank of England does. The Banks would thus be a species of commercial barometer for the trading community, and, as in Eng land, indicate the condition of the commercial atmosphere, and give timely warning of coming storms, or the contrary.

To Question 2.—In the above named particular, they are too restrictive, but in other respects, not generally so.

To Question 3.—$600,000 I consider as small an amount as safely can be granted in a charter to any Bank, one third paid up before going into operation.

To Question 4.—6,000,000 (six million dollars) should be the maximum amount of capital granted in any charter.

To Question 5.—The present restrictions are wise in many respects, they are in some inconsistent, however. Banks should not be prevented, when discounting paper, from strengthening the transaction by taking collateral security in the shape of Government Bonds, Bank Stocks (other than the Bank making loan) and such other first class securities (always excepting real estate) as your committee may deem safe and undoubted.

To Question 6.—Practically, to prove the measure so far as it went a safe and salutary one. Banks, although permitted to charge 7 per cent. by law, did not do so—the money market being under that rate.

To Question 7.—Undoubtedly they would. The interests of commerce have ever been injured by all such restrictions ; they have no effect on real value of money, and only serve to injure the poorer classes by giving to first-class paper a Bank monopoly in discounts.

To Question 8 —Not more than its own paid up capital as at present.

To Question 9.— One to four, or four and a half.

To Question 10.—This Bank (the City Bank, Montreal) commenced in the year 1833 with a subscribed capital of $800,000, and one-fourth paid up.

To Question 11.—In 1842, $400,000 ; reduced $300,000 in 1849 ; and again increased $300,000 in 1854 ; making its present capital $1,200,000.

To Question 12.—The City Bank paid one bonus of 3 per cent., and, including this, the average dividends paid since its establishment have been $5\frac{1}{2}$ per cent per annum, and taking off $240,000, capital written off to cover losses in 1849, the average dividend would be reduced to $4\frac{3}{4}$ per cent. per annum.

To Question 13.—1834, $4,810 18 ; 1835, $8,793 03 ; 1836, $20,795 23 ; 1837, $16,183 27 ; 1838, $11,467 72 ; 1839, $20,141 83 ; 1840, $36,747 15 ; 1841, $46,304 13 ; 1842, $61,444 57 ; 1843, $33,032 00 ; 1844, $38,269 99 ; 1845, $52,000 00 ; 1846, $66,000 00 ; 1847, $86,100 00 ; 1848, $111,500 00. This rest was all lost, and in addition to it $300,000 of the capital to cover losses to this date. 1849, $12,500 00 ; 1850, $29,825 27 ; 1851, $64.656 20 ; 1852, $10,775 27 ; 1853, $96,179 20 ; 1854, $100,574 43 ; 1855, $96,216 47 ; 1856, $138,614 68 ; 1857, $162,312 88 ; 1858, $140,243 95.

To Question 14.—Along with other Banks here, the City Bank suspended specie payments on May 1837 (the year of the Canadian Rebellion) and resumed again in May 1838—a second suspension took place by order of the Special Council in the fall of 1838, along with other Banks.

To Question 15.—Not being connected with the institution then, cannot say.

To Question 16.—Same answer as last.

To Question 17.—So far as I can remember, the tendency was to increase exchanges against us largely, to raise prices of commodities in proportion to the premium on specie, to confine Bank accommodation to parties indebted to Banks when suspension took place, and generally to produce an inflated and unnatural condition of commercial matters.

To Question 18.—None.

To Question 19.—Not desirable.

To Question 20.—I think that a Provincial gold coinage might be of advantage in checking a speculative demand for specie during a money crisis; heretofore serious inconvenience has been felt from foreigners making a trade of " running" on our Banks during a panic, and carrying off the gold to New York for sale as a mere matter of speculation. Had such demands been met by a provincial gold coinage, the trade in this way would, no doubt, to a large extent, have been checked. The new coinage should be in pieces of *one pound currency five dollars* differently shaped from the pound, and tens, twentys, &c., &c., dollar pieces.

To Question 21.—None that I can see.

To Question 22.—Over-trading and adventurous speculation; a short crop, (or alarm in some other commercial community) generally acting as the spark to spring the mine—The power possessed by the Bank of England of regulating the rate of discount according to the demand for money is a great safety valve for preventing commercial explosions of this character; our Banks should possess similar powers here.

To Question 23.—Land speculation in Western Canada; the iniquitous loans to various Municipalities under the Municipal Loan Fund Act inflating everything, and drawing the community from habits of patient industry, no doubt contributed largely to produce the serious depression of trade and general derangement in that portion of the province which now exists and has so long existed.

To Question 24.—Yes, make money free.

(Signed,)   WILLIAM WORKMAN,
President of the City Bank.

Montreal, 2nd April, 1859.

The following answers received :—

(*From the Cashier of the City Bank,*) *Montreal.*

To Question 1.—In most particulars they generally do.

To Question 2.—The charters appear to me to be too restrictive in some particulars. I would here take leave to remark that charters are too unguardedly granted.

To Question 3.—I am of opinion that no Bank should be chartered having a less capital than $800,000, and one-fourth the amount should be paid in before such Bank is permitted to commence its business.

To Question 4.—Yes. I think the capital of no Bank should be permitted to exceed $6,000,000.

To Question 5.—I am of opinion it would be advisable to authorize the Banks when discounting notes and cashing drafts or bills of exchange, to take collateral securities by bills of lading, Government or Municipal bonds, Bank stocks (other than the Bank making the loan), and such other securities as your Committee may think advisable to add, omitting fixed property, except by mortgage and hypothèque, by way of additional security for debts contracted, as is now regulated by the charters.

To Question 6.—The effect of the late increased rate of interest which Banks are permitted to charge has been practically to show that no apprehension need be felt in extending to Banks the same privilege as is enjoyed by others; as, although permitted to charge 7 per cent, the Banks in this part of the Province, as a general rule, have only charged, since the passing of the Act referred to, six per cent.

To Question 7.—I decidedly think both would be promoted by the removal of all restrictions as regards rates of interest.

To Question 8.—The maximum which a Bank should be allowed to issue of its own paper ought not to exceed the amount of its own capital paid up.

To Question 9.—About one-fourth.

To Question 10.—The Bank (City Bank, Montreal,) commenced operations in the year 1833, with a subscribed capital of $800,000, and $200,000 paid up.

To Question 11.—The augmentation of capital has been since the first charter was granted $400,000 in the year 1842 ; was reduced $300,000 in 1849, and again increased $300,000 in 1854, summing up its present capital of $1,200,000.

To Question 12.—The average dividend (one bonus of 3 per cent. included) paid since the establishment of the Bank, has been at the rate of 5½ per cent. per annum. From this, however, may be deducted the sum of $240,000 for the reduction made in the capital stock, which would lessen the average dividend to 4¾ per cent per annum.

To Question 13.—The amount of the Bank Rest was as follows:

In the year 1834	$4,810 18
1835	8,793 03
1836	20,795 23
1837	16,183 27
1838	11,467 72
1839	20,141 83
1840	36,747 15
1841	46,304 13
1842	61,444 37
1843	33,032 00

1844	38,269 99
1845	52,000 00
1846	66,000 00
1847	86,100 00
1848	115,500 00

In addition to this rest in 1848, $300,000 was written off from the capital under the authority of Parliament to cover losses to this date.

1849	12,500 00
1850	29,825 27
1851	64.656 20
1852	10,775 27
1853	36 179 20
1854	100,574 43
1855	96,2:6 47
1856	138,614 68
1857	162,312 88
1858	140,243 95

To Question 14.—The Bank with other institutions here suspended specie payments in the month of May 1837 (the year of the Rebellion) and resumed again in the same month of the following year 1838.

To Question 15.—At the time of the suspension the liabilities of the Bank were $519,761 60. Specie in vault $63,564 67. Discounted paper $1,216,209 78.

To Question 16.—As I was not an officer of the Bank at the time, I cannot say what the state of the discount sheet was. On reference to the Books I find the amount of the Bank paper in circulation at the resumption of specie payments to have been $451, 614 00.

To Question 17.—Not being an officer of the Bank at the time, I cannot say what effect was produced by the suspension and resumption of specie payments on the business transactions of the country.

To Question 18.—I have no suggestion to offer with reference to either.

To Question 19.—In my opinion it would not be advisable to make silver a legal tender to a larger amount than it is at present.

To Question 20.—I do not think a provincial gold coinage would be of any advantage.

To Question 21.—I am not prepared to say that any alteration is desirable in the present mode of receiving or paying gold.

To Question 22.—This question is of too momentous a character, requiring much time and research, to be satisfactorily answered here.

To Question 23.—Same as given to question 22.

To Question 24.—I am of opinion that over-trading can be checked, and commercial depression, not perhaps alleviated, but in a great measure prevented by legislative enactment granting to the Banking institutions the power to demand at all times such rate of discount as they may see is necessary to check speculation, and give timely warning of the approach of difficulty which would be sure to lead to an immediate contraction of business and otherwise be attended with most important results to commerce and the well being of the country at large.

(Signed,)   F. MACCULLOCH,
Cashier.

City Bank,
    Montreal, 29th March, 1859.

———

The following answers received—

(From the Cashier of la Banque du Peuple,) Montreal.

To Question 1.—I have an objection to the Banks being compelled to invest $\frac{1}{10}$th of their capital in Government securities, it is unnecessarily locking up capital which ought to be employed in commercial transactions and developing the resources of the country.

To Question 2.—I think not.

To Question 3.—A capital paid up of not less than £100,000.

To Question 4.—Yes, large capitals are dangerous, I think, £500,000 as large an amount as any Bank ought to have.

To Question 5.—I think the present restrictions wise and sufficient.

To Question 6.—Little or no change has taken place in the rate of interest charged by the Banks; the regular customers have only been charged at the rate of 6 per cent. per annum.

To Question 8.—A Bank should not be permitted to circulate her own notes for more than two-thirds of the amount of her paid up capital.

To Question 9.—In my opinion Banks ought to be obliged to have at all times in their vaults, in specie and bullion, one-fourth the amount of the paper (Bank Notes) they may have in circulation.

To Question 10.—In 1845 with a subscribed capital of £200,000, of which £113,487 15s. 9d. was paid in.

To Question 11.—Our present capital is £300,000 authorised by the 14th Vic., cap. 43; the amount of capital paid in is £268,487 10s. 0d. currency.

To Question 12.—We have paid 28 dividends since 1st March, 1845, amounting together to 87½ per cent.

To Question 13.—

		£	s.	d.
Rest 1st of March 1846		1,368	8	3
"	1847	5,081	18	3
"	1848	6,960	5	10
"	1849	5,617	5	9
"	1850	4,634	6	0
"	1851	4,602	10	4

"	1852..........................	3,188	19	7
"	1853..........................	9,540	19	10
"	1854..........................	19,812	13	7
"	1855..........................	30,586	14	1
"	1856..........................	32,700	13	5
"	1857..........................	38,446	15	11
"	1858..........................	41,386	6	9
"	1859..........................	41,389	1	4

To Question 14.—No.

To Question 17.—Unfavorable effects, as all unnatural expansions and contractions must ever be productive of.

To Question 18.—No, I am satisfied with both.

To Question 19.—I think English shillings and six pennys, ought to be reduced in value about 2½ per cent, and then the shilling allowed to be a legal tender to the extent of £100 currency.

To Question 20.—I think not, the current and legal coins of the United States of America are the best gold and silver coins we can have.

To Question 21.—I think not.

To Question 24.—I think not.

B. H. LEMOINE,

Cashier.

La Banque du Peuple,
   Montreal 31st March, 1859.

————

The following answers received—

   (*From the President of the Gore Bank,*) *Hamilton.*

To Question 1. I have not perused the Charters of all the Banks.

To Question 2. Answer as above.

To Question 3. About $609,000 or $800,000.

To Question 4. I think there should be.

To Question 5. Banks should be allowed to lend money as they please, as is the case in England.

To Question 6. No benefit visibly yet to the Banks; there is nothing in the country to buy money with.

To Question 7. Certainly; remove all restrictions on money and trade, and money will then be abundant.

To Question 8. Bank Notes at present are returned at once.

To Question 9. About one to five.

To Question 10.   In 1836.   Capital then $400,000.

To Question 11.   Doubled in 1854.

To Question 12.   Several years 6 per cent., several years seven, and several years eight.

To Question 13.

1837, May 31, £1242 0 9	1845, £7563 14 7	1853, £19776 10 4
1838, 1595 12 3	1846, 9267 15 11	1854, 7794 13 11
1839, 2964 5 8	1847, 9859 7 9	1855, 22340 8 3
1840, 5192 2 5	1848, 13231 2 7	1856, 39863 9 1
1841, 7156 6 8	1849, 6666 5 2	1857, 27984 7 7
1842, 10481 12 8	1850, 5300 10 1	1858, $127417 08
1843, 9557 2 0	1851, 9509 4 8	1859, } 120831 74
1844, 5636 17 4	1852, 14599 12 7	March 31, }

To Question 14.   Yes ; by order of Government in March '38, and resumed in November '39.

To Question 15.   Notes in circulation £13101 10 0
Deposits, ... 14743 11 9
Gold and Silver, ... 21147 3 8
Notes discounted, ... 48632 18 3

To Question 16.   Notes discounted 63004 3 6
Notes in circulation, ... 46439 0 0

To Question 17.   Do not recollect so far back.

To Question 18.   None.

To Question 19.   Do not know.

To Question 20.   No consequence.

To Question 21.   Do.

To Question 24.   Remove all restrictions on Trade, Commerce, and Money, and they will protect themselves.

A. STEVEN,
President.

Gore Bank, Hamilton, 15th April, 1859.

The following answers received—

(*From the Cashier of the Molson's Bank,*) *Montreal.*

To Question 1.—Having seen but a few of the bank charters, I am unable to give an opinion upon them generally.

To Question 2.—Such of the charters as I have seen appear too restrictive as regards the nature of the securities upon which banks are authorised to grant discounts, as well as in the restrictions on acquiring real estate on which they may have mortgages.

To Question 3.—I am not prepared to say that under certain circumstances it would be impolitic to charter banks with a minimum capital of $400,000, but in such cases they should not be allowed to have any agencies—when agencies are allowed, the minimum should be $1,000,000.

To Question 4.—Yes.

To Question 5.—In some instances they should be removed as stated in answer to question No. 2.

To Question 6.—It has enabled the bank to discount occasionally for persons who did not keep accounts with it, charging them the increased rate.

To Question 7.—I am of opinion that they would.

To Question 8.—The amount of its paid up capital.

To Question 9.—I do not think that it would desirable to fix a proportion—none exists at present, and I am not aware of any inconvenience having arisen in consequence.

To Question 10.—In the year 1855 with a capital of one million dollars.

To Question 11.—None.

To Question 12.—It has always paid dividends (semi-annually) at the rate of 8 per cent. per annum.

To Question 13.—The rest was, 1st year, $7,963 43.
2nd "   21,197 03.
3rd   "   36,000 00.

To Question 14.—No.

To Question 18.—No.

To Question 19.—I do not think that it would be desirable.

To Question 20.—There does not appear to me to be any necessity for it just now.

To Question 21.—The present mode seems to work very well.

To Questions 22 *and* 23. It would be impossible within the limits of this paper to answer these questions.

To Question 24.—I do not see how Legislative action can be brought to bear so as to check overtrading.

WM. SACHE,
Cashier.

Molson's Bank,
     Montreal, 30th March, 1859.

The following answers received—

To Question 1.—The objects which it is presumed any Legislature have in view in chartering a Bank are the following.—First, To provide an institution in which money may be safely deposited by the Government or by individuals; and Second, To provide for the issue of a safe circulating medium other than gold and silver, and more convenient. The public safety is the only proper ground for legislative interference with the business of banking, and every privilege or restriction should have this object in view. This may be secured in two ways—indirectly, by such regulations as shall ensure stability—directly, by restrictions on doing business in an unsafe manner. Both are aimed at in most of the charters hitherto granted. With respect to the former point—that of stability—it seems to be fairly provided for in many of them by the high minimum capital, both subscribed and paid up, required before commencing business. The regulations on the latter point, as for example, the limitation of the privilege of circulating notes,—the prohibiting discount to directors beyond a certain sum,—the forbidding to declare dividends out of capital, together with the obligation to publish periodical statements, are generally calculated to effect the object. The regulations under both heads are however open to considerable improvement in all the charters (see Answer to Question No. 2), and it should be said that most of those lately granted are so extremely defective as scarcely to afford any protection.

To Question 2.—The Charters are too restrictive in the following:

1. In the prohibition to discount on the security of bills of lading and warehouse receipts; no more legitimate method of employing Bank capital or one more strictly within the line of business can be named.
2. In the prohibition to raise loans, which strictly interpreted as it stands, might be held to prevent a Bank from obtaining an advance in case of emergency.
The Charters are too unguarded in the following. First,—In not securing the *bonâ fide* payment of the minimum amount of capital required to be paid up before business can be commenced. This might be remedied to a certain extent, either by requiring that the amount be deposited with the Bank at which the Government account is kept; or by requiring that the sum shall be held in specie, and actually counted by a Government officer. This course, though only an approximation to absolute security, is the best that can be adopted to effect the object (apart from an inquisitorial method which would provoke evasion) for although it does not prevent the amount being borrowed temporarily and lodged or held at the time of commencing, to be repaid immediately, it does secure that the parties having the direction of the Bank shall be persons of standing and responsibility, for none but such could obtain so large a sum as would be required (see Question No. 3) even for a day. Second,—In allowing the Debentures upon which a certain portion of circulation is based to remain in the custody of the Bank, for there is nothing to prevent a Bank hypothecating them, and thus destroying the security of such portion of circulation as is based upon them. If Debentures be used as a basis of circulation at all, they should be lodged in the hands of the Government.

3. The Charters are particularly loose in allowing specie and debentures to form a basis of circulation *in addition to capital*. For specie and debentures can only be obtained in two ways, by purchasing them with capital or with deposits. To obtain debentures or to hold specie, a Bank must either employ its own funds,

or the fund deposited with it by others. In the former case, so much of the *capital is displaced* as is invested or held thus ; that is so much of the capital consists of specie and debentures. They form constituent portions of the capital, and it is therefore absurd to treat them as something independent of, or distinct from it. On the other hand, the specie and debentures of a Bank may have been procured with the funds deposited with it. In this case so much of money deposited is held in specie and debentures. The Bank is already liable to pay this money and it is therefore absurd to base an additionald liability upon it as a security.

4. Charters should all contain a provision for winding up the business when a certain portion of the capital has been lost, or after stopping payment ; or this might be embraced in a general Act on the subject. It might be expedient to appoint a Government officer, whose functions should correspond with those of the Superintendent of the Bank Department in the State of New York, to whose custody debentures should be committed, who should have charge of periodical statements, and whose certificate of the payment of the necessary amount of capital should be required before a Bank could commence business.

5. Directors should be required to have at least $4000 paid up before election.

6. At least two-thirds of the stock should be held by parties in the Province as security to the creditors, in the event of the clause of double liability being required to be enforced.

To Question 3.—When circulation rests upon capital and not upon actual security held by Government, the capital should be of sufficient amount to ensure stability. Now stability depends mainly on good management, and good management can only be had by liberal remuneration. This again can only be afforded by a certain amount of capital, and calculations would show that $200,000 paid up is the lowest sum on which a well managed Bank can profitably commence. An adequate capital, moreover, will be a means of securing the services of such persons as Directors as have proved their ability to manage the funds of other persons by accumulating a considerable sum of their own.

It should be made obligatory to raise the full amount of the subscribed capital within a limited period, and the minimum of this might be fixed at $1,000,000, in case the head office of the institution were to be located in any one of the three principal cities, and at $400,000, if the centre is to be at any other point

Even when circulation is secured by pledge of Government stocks, the safety of depositors and the convenience of the public require that the capital of a Bank (issuing notes) should be of considerable amount, for nothing more deranges the course of business than the frequent stoppage of Banks, and experience has shown that ephemeral institutions, easily made and easily broken, are an injury, and not a benefit, to a community.

To Question 4.—If by this question is meant,—Should a Bank when its minimum is fixed be allowed to go on at pleasure ? the answer would be, No. A Bank ought not to be chartered without a fixed subscribed capital, and the amount of this should depend on the point which is to be the centre of operations. If at that point a sum of $100,000 in cash cannot be raised with a certain prospect of increase to $400,000 within a limited period, an independant Bank has no business there at all. The business would be better done by an agency of a larger institution. But if this sum or more can be raised, the maximum of capital should have reference to the requirements of the district tributary to and dependent upon that centre.

If, however, by this question is meant,—Should there be a maximum beyond which no Bank whatever should be allowed to increase its capital? the answer to this again would be, No. For the requirements of business offer the only proper limit to the capital of a Bank, and the directors and stockholders of any institution are the best judges, whether in their case additional capital can be profitably employed. Other considerations than the requirements of business and the safety of the public have no right to be taken into account in this connection.

To Question 5.—The only notification required is suggested in the answer to question 2.

To Question 6.—Nothing of any importance.

To Question 7.—Yes.

To Question 8—Three-fourths of the capital is sufficient.

To Question 9.—This question can scarcely be answered intelligently in its present shape, for a Bank has other liabilities payable at call besides circulation and other available assets besides specie, but it may be said generally that the line of safety will vary with the circumstances of the money market. In times of pressure a Bank will endeavour to keep a specie reserve to the extent of one-third or one fourth of its circulation, but when money is easy, one sixth or one seventh would be held sufficient.

To Question 10.—1856. $109,700.

To Question 11.—The capital is now $501,050, the augmentation having been by half-yearly calls of 10 per cent. and by subscriptions of additional Stock.

To Question 12.—Two half-yearly dividends have been declared at the rate of 10 per cent. per annum, and three subsequently at the rate of eight per cent. per annum.

To Question 13.—July 1857, $19,202.28. July 1858, $20,000.

To Questions 14, 15, 16 and 17.—These four questions are answered by the statement that the Bank has never suspended specie payments.

To Question 18.—Retaining the obligation to pay specie if called upon, weekly settlements had better be left to mutual arrangement as at present.

To Question 19.—Silver ought not to be made a legal tender to an amount which would be unwieldy. And as so small a sum in silver is unwieldy, it does not appear that any useful purpose would be answered by increasing the amount beyond which it may be tendered at present.

To Question 20.—Of no advantage whatever.

To Question 21.—No.

To Question 22.—To answer this question properly would require a treatise, but gen rally they may be referred to abuse of credit. Credit is only legitimate when based upon something actually realised, but when based upon the prospective profits of future years, it is illegitimate and entails loss; the consequence of this is want of confidence more or less severe and depression.

To *Question* 23.—Yes.

To *Question* 24.—By placing restrictions on Banks, the Legislature can check over-trading and illegitimate speculation to a certain extent, but the following paragraph from a Report of a Committee of the House of Lords on the causes of commercial Distress in 1848, is so much in point in this connection, that it may with propriety be quoted as a closing remark. "The best banking system may be defeated by imperfect management; and on the other hand, the evils of an imperfect banking system may be greatly mitigated, if not overcome by prudence, caution and Resolution.

(Signed,)   A. CAMERON,

Bank of Toronto.   Cashier.

The following answers received—

(*From the Cashier of the International Bank of Canada,*) *Toronto.*

To *Question* 1.— I think they do.

To *Question* 2.—I think they do not.

To *Question* 3.—$500,000 for Country Banks, and $1,000,000 for City Banks.

To *Question* 4.—As above named.

To *Question* 5 —They should be qualified, by so doing they will aid commercial transactions.

To *Question* 6.—I think the effect has been beneficial.

To *Question* 7.—I think they would be generally promoted.

To *Question* 8.—Not beyond its paid up capital.

To *Question* 9.—At least one fourth.

To *Question* 10.—In 1858, $1,000,000.

To *Question* 11.—None.

To *Questions* 12 *and* 13.—None; this Bank has been in operation too short a time.

To *Question* 14.—No.

To *Question* 18.—I have none.

To *Question* 19.—I think it would not.

To *Question* 20.—No.

To *Question* 21.—None is desirable.

To *Question* 22.—Over-trading and reckless speculation.

To *Question* 23.—Yes, to an alarming extent.

To *Question* 24.—It cannot be.

(Signed,)   J. MACKELL,

International Bank of Canada,   Cashier.
    March 31, 1859.

The following answers received—

(From the Vice-President of the Niagara District Bank,) St. Catharines.

To Question 1.—In general they do. Would rather they remain as they are than hazard new legislation.

To Question 2.—To both of these questions I should answer—No.

To Question 3.—There should be two classes—City and Country Banks. The former with not less than $1,000,000—and the latter $400,000 capital. Caution should be used in granting charters, as numerous Banks are undoubtedly injurious to public interests.

To Question 4.—$1,000,000 Country.
                           $4,000,000 City.

To Question 5.—In addition to present securities Banks should have the privilege of granting discounts on the security of Bills of Lading and Warehouse Receipts of Produce.

To Question 6.—So far I think it has worked to the advantage both of the Banks and the public at large.

To Question 7.—Not at present.

To Question 8.—As it now is.

To Question 9.—The system at present adopted by the Banks regulating this should, I think, be continued.

To Question 10.—In 1854, under the Free Banking Act, with a capital of $200,000.

To Question 11.—Obtained charter in 1855 with an augmentation of $800,000 capital.

To Question 12.—One at 6 per cent. per annum; two at 7; five at 8; two at 10, and one bonus at 10, payable in stock.

To Question 13.—1855 December 31 .... $15,926 87
                           1856   " 34,107 96
                           1857   " 52,315 04
                           1858   " 25,996 92

To Question 14.—No.

To Question 18.—The denominations of notes now issued appear to suit the requirements of trade, and the mode of settlement of balances can be better arranged by the Banks themselves.

To Question 19.—In order to keep up the character of our circulation, redemptions should be made in gold, or its equivalent in silver.

To Question 20.—Commercially, it would be of no advantage—Nationally, would prefer it.

To Question 21.—Prefer it as it is.

To Question 22.—Recklessness of expenditure, over-trading, and land speculations.

To Question 23.—Yes, more than any other country during the past five years.

To Question 24.—No.

THOS. B. MERRITT,
Vice-president.

Niagara District Bank,
St. Catharines, 19th March, 1859.

———

The following answers received—

(*From the Bank of Clifton*), *Clifton.*

To Question 1. Yes.

To Question 2. No, not if faithfully carried out.

To Question 3. £250,000.

To Question 4. No.

To Question 5. Retaining.

To Question 8. Not beyond paid up capital.

To Question 9. One fifth.

To Question 10. 1854 under free Banking Act, and chartered to £250,000 in 1856.

To Question 11. None.

To Question 12. Eight per cent. and wound up after the death of Mr. Zimmerman.

To Question 14. No.

To Question 20. Yes, 5, 10 and 20.

To Question 21. By tale.

Memorandum.—The Bank Charter should not, in my opinion, be granted unless the parties or Stockholders asking for it have first subscribed *bonâ fide* for the Capital Stock of the same, and such list to be presented with the petition asking for an Act of incorporation, the fact that the first instalment having been paid into some one of our present Chartered Banks, being, in my judgment, no security to the public. And further, indiscriminately granting charters will have a bad tendency upon our Banks already in operation.

The principal of granting charters is, in my opinion, correct, but the only security is in the *list of Stockholders.*

JOSEPH A. WOODRUFF,
President, Bank of Clifton.

ANSWERS RECEIVED

FROM THE

FOLLOWING BANKS.

TORONTO:

PRINTED BY JOHN LOVELL, YONGE STREET.